NFL TEAM STORIES

The Story of the

BALTIMORE RAVENS

By Diane Bailey

Kaleidoscope
Minneapolis, MN

The Quest for Discovery Never Ends

·······································

This edition first published in 2021 by Kaleidoscope Publishing, Inc.

No part of this publication may be reproduced in whole or in part without written permission of the publisher.

For information regarding permission, write to
Kaleidoscope Publishing, Inc.
6012 Blue Circle Drive
Minnetonka, MN 55343

Library of Congress Control Number
2020933596

ISBN
978-1-64519-220-6 (library bound)
978-1-64519-288-6 (ebook)

Text copyright © 2021 by Kaleidoscope Publishing, Inc. All-Star Sports, Bigfoot Books, and associated logos are trademarks and/or registered trademarks of Kaleidoscope Publishing, Inc.

Printed in the United States of America.

Bigfoot lurks within one of the images in this book. It's up to you to find him!

TABLE OF CONTENTS

Kickoff!... 4

Chapter 1: Ravens History... 6

Chapter 2: Ravens All-Time Greats 16

Chapter 3: Ravens Superstars 22

Beyond the Book.. 28
Research Ninja.. 29
Further Resources 30
Glossary 31
Index 32
Photo Credits... 32
About the Author... 32

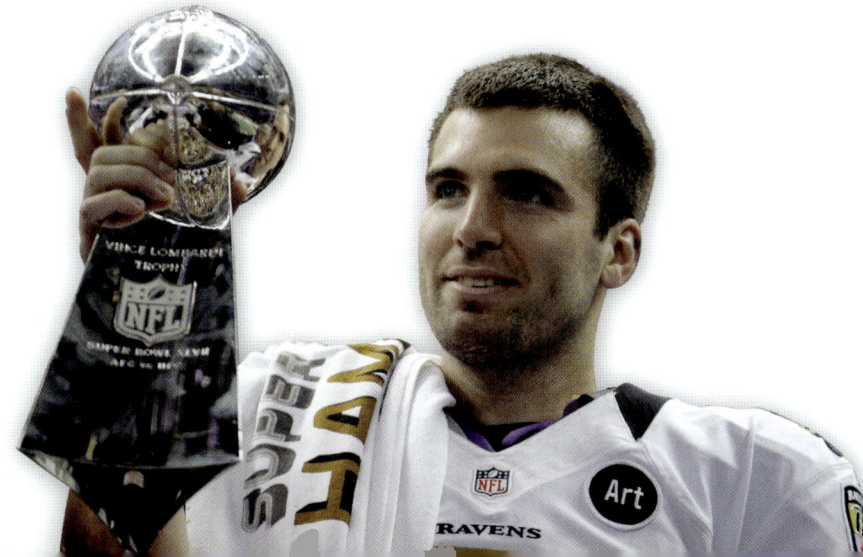

KICKOFF!

What is that giant bird doing on the field? Don't worry, he has a job to do. That's Poe. He's the mascot of the Baltimore Ravens. When he takes the field, it's time for fans to cheer. The Ravens have given their fans a lot to cheer for. The team has won a Super Bowl.

Today's Ravens have some of the NFL's most exciting young players. In 2019, they came close to reaching the Super Bowl again.

Poe wants more things to cheer for. Let's meet the Ravens and find out what all the squawking is about!

Chapter 1
Ravens History

Football has a long history in Baltimore. The Baltimore Colts played from 1953 to 1983. In 1958, the Colts played the New York Giants. It was the NFL Championship Game. Quarterback Johnny Unitas took the Colts to a win in **overtime**! The game was one of the first to be on TV. People all over the country watched. It helped make football popular.

The Colts moved to Indianapolis in 1984. Fans were sorry to see them go. In 1996, the NFL decided to add another team. Baltimore was chosen to get it. Football was back with the Ravens!

NAME THAT TEAM

A famous author named Edgar Allan Poe once lived in Baltimore. He wrote a poem called "The Raven." The people of Baltimore wanted to honor the city's history. They voted to call their new football team the Ravens.

FUN FACT
Vinny Testaverde scored the first TD in Ravens history in 1996.

The Ravens had losing seasons their first three years. Head coach Brian Billick came on board in 1999. He turned the Ravens into a top-notch team.

Some great players helped the team come together. Jamal Lewis was a standout running back. Jonathan Ogden was a solid tackle. On defense, linebackers Ray Lewis and Peter Boulware were important. In one game against the Minnesota Vikings, Boulware **sacked** the Vikings' quarterback four times!

The 2000 season was a big success. The Ravens went to the Super Bowl. Baltimore's great defense was too tough for the New York Giants. The Giants scored one touchdown the whole game. The Ravens won with a final score of 34-7.

Brandon Stokely pulls away from Jason Sehorn to score a big Super Bowl TD.

In 2008, John Harbaugh took over as head coach. **Rookie** quarterback Joe Flacco also started that year. He led the team to the playoffs. They did not make the Super Bowl, though.

In 2013, the Ravens were up for the division championship. They faced the Denver Broncos. Most people thought the Broncos would win. With less than a minute left in the game, the Broncos were up by a touchdown. Then Flacco threw a 70-yard pass to receiver Jacoby Jones. He ran for a touchdown. It tied the game! The Ravens' Justin Tucker kicked a field goal in overtime. The Ravens went back to the Super Bowl that season. (See page 14.)

Ravens QB Joe Flacco celebrates after throwing a game-tying TD pass.

The Ravens struggled the next few years. They could not make the playoffs. By 2018 they were back on their feet. Their offense and defense were both in the NFL's top ten. In 2019, they were even better. Lamar Jackson became one of the NFL's best players. The Ravens set an NFL team record with 3,296 rushing yards.

Their 14–2 record was best in the NFL. Sadly, they were upset by Tennessee in the playoffs. With great Ravens talent, more good seasons are ahead!

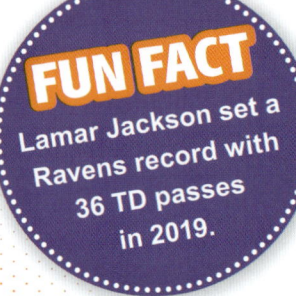

FUN FACT

Lamar Jackson set a Ravens record with 36 TD passes in 2019.

TIMELINE OF THE BALTIMORE RAVENS

1996: The Baltimore Ravens are founded.

2001: The Ravens play in their first Super Bowl. They defeat the New York Giants, 34-7.

2008: John Harbaugh becomes the head coach.

2013: Baltimore takes home its second Super Bowl win, against the San Francisco 49ers.

2018: The Ravens play in their first Pro Football Hall of Fame game. They beat the Chicago Bears, 17-16.

2019: The Ravens post their best regular-season record, 14-2.

TWO-TIME CHAMPS

In 2013, the Ravens played the San Francisco 49ers in the Super Bowl. It was a special game for head coach John Harbaugh. His brother, Jim, coached the 49ers. Brother-vs.-brother coaches had never happened before! Both teams had been to the Super Bowl before. Neither had ever lost. This would be a big game!

Quarterback Joe Flacco led the Ravens to a strong start. The 49ers fought back hard. Baltimore held on. When the clock ran out, the score was 34-31 for Baltimore. The Ravens had done it again!

Baltimore coach John Harbaugh spoke before the game next to his brother, Niners coach Jim Harbaugh.

Joe Flacco holds up the Lombardi Trophy.

Chapter 2
Ravens All-Time Greats

When the Ravens started in 1996, they had to build a team from scratch. They got some good picks in their first **draft**. Left tackle Jonathan Ogden was at the top of the list. His job was to protect the quarterback. He also had to clear a path through the defensive line for runners. "Oggie" became a Hall of Fame star.

Jonathan Ogden

Ray Lewis

The Ravens also added linebacker Ray Lewis. Some people thought he was too small to play that position. They changed their minds soon! Lewis was not afraid to make tough tackles. When Ravens won the Super Bowl in 2001, Lewis was the game's MVP. Baltimore's next Super Bowl win was 12 years later. Lewis was still with the team! That was his last game. He went out on the biggest win of them all.

Running back Jamal Lewis was a rookie during the 2001 Super Bowl. By 2003, he was a standout player. Fans just said, *"Give the ball to Jamal."* That was the goal of the offense. In a game against the Cleveland Browns, Lewis carried the ball 30 times. He gained a total of 295 yards. That set an NFL record for a single game.

Ed Reed came on board as a **safety** in 2002. Reed had a nose for the football. He had 64 career **interceptions**. He took seven back for touchdowns. In 2003, he blocked a punt against the Seattle Seahawks. Then he grabbed the ball and ran for a touchdown. The Ravens came from behind to tie the game. Then they won in overtime! Reed had great instincts. Now he is in the Pro Football Hall of Fame.

Ed Reed

Jamal Lewis

Quarterback Joe Flacco was not sure he was good enough to play in the NFL. He had to prove himself. In Flacco's rookie year, the Ravens' main quarterback was out. Could Flacco do the job? The Ravens played the Cincinnati Bengals in their opening game. Flacco ran the football for a 38-yard touchdown. The Ravens notched a win! Flacco took his team all the way to the playoffs.

Defensive end Terrell Suggs ("T-Sizzle") really sizzled on the field. Blockers tried all kinds of ways to stop him. He always found a way through. In 2011, he was picked as the NFL's best defensive player.

Joe Flacco

RAVENS
RECORDS

These players piled up the best stats in Ravens history. The numbers are career records through the 2019 season.

Total TDs: Jamal Lewis, 47

TD Passes: Joe Flacco, 212

Passing Yards: Joe Flacco, 38,245

Rushing Yards: Jamal Lewis, 7,801

Receptions: Derrick Mason, 471

Points: Matt Stover, 1,464

Sacks: Terrell Suggs, 132.5

Chapter 3
Ravens Superstars

Lamar Jackson was going to be a star. It was just a question of when. He won the **Heisman Trophy** as a junior at Louisville. The Ravens took him with the 32nd pick of the 2018 NFL Draft. He didn't start right away, though.

As the backup, he kept working hard. When he got his chance, he took off. He has become one of the best players in the NFL. When he gets the ball, opponents don't know what to do. Jackson can pass very well. He is also a great runner. How do you stop him?

In 2019, few teams could. He led Baltimore to a 14-2 record. He also set an all-time NFL record for quarterbacks. He ran for 1,206 yards. He also led the NFL with 36 touchdown passes! Jackson is a one-of-a-kind double-threat!

FUN FACT
Lamar Jackson got all 50 first-place votes for the NFL MVP in 2019.

Jackson was part of the Ravens' record-setting offense in 2019. Mark Ingram was another big part. In 2011, the running back also won the Heisman Trophy. He rumbled for 1,018 yards in 2019. He scored 10 touchdowns, too. Ingram gives the Ravens a powerful weapon at the goal line.

Mark Ingram

Matt Judon

Offensive lineman Marshal Yanda helped Jackson and Ingram get room to run. Yanda is one of the best guards in the NFL. In one game he blocked three defenders in a single play! Yanda has been with the team a long time. When he was new, **veterans** like Jonathan Ogden helped him. Now the rookies come to Yanda for advice.

The Ravens defense has a lot of top young players. In 2019, linebacker Matt Judon stepped up. He had 9.5 sacks. That led the team. Opposing QBs don't like to see him coming their way!

The Ravens depend on kicker Justin Tucker. He is the most accurate kicker ever in the NFL.

In a game against the Detroit Lions, Tucker was the only Raven who scored. He kicked six field goals. The last one was 61 yards long. He got all 18 of the Ravens' points.

The Ravens are one of the newest teams in the NFL. They are also one of the best. Their fans expect great things. The Ravens deliver!

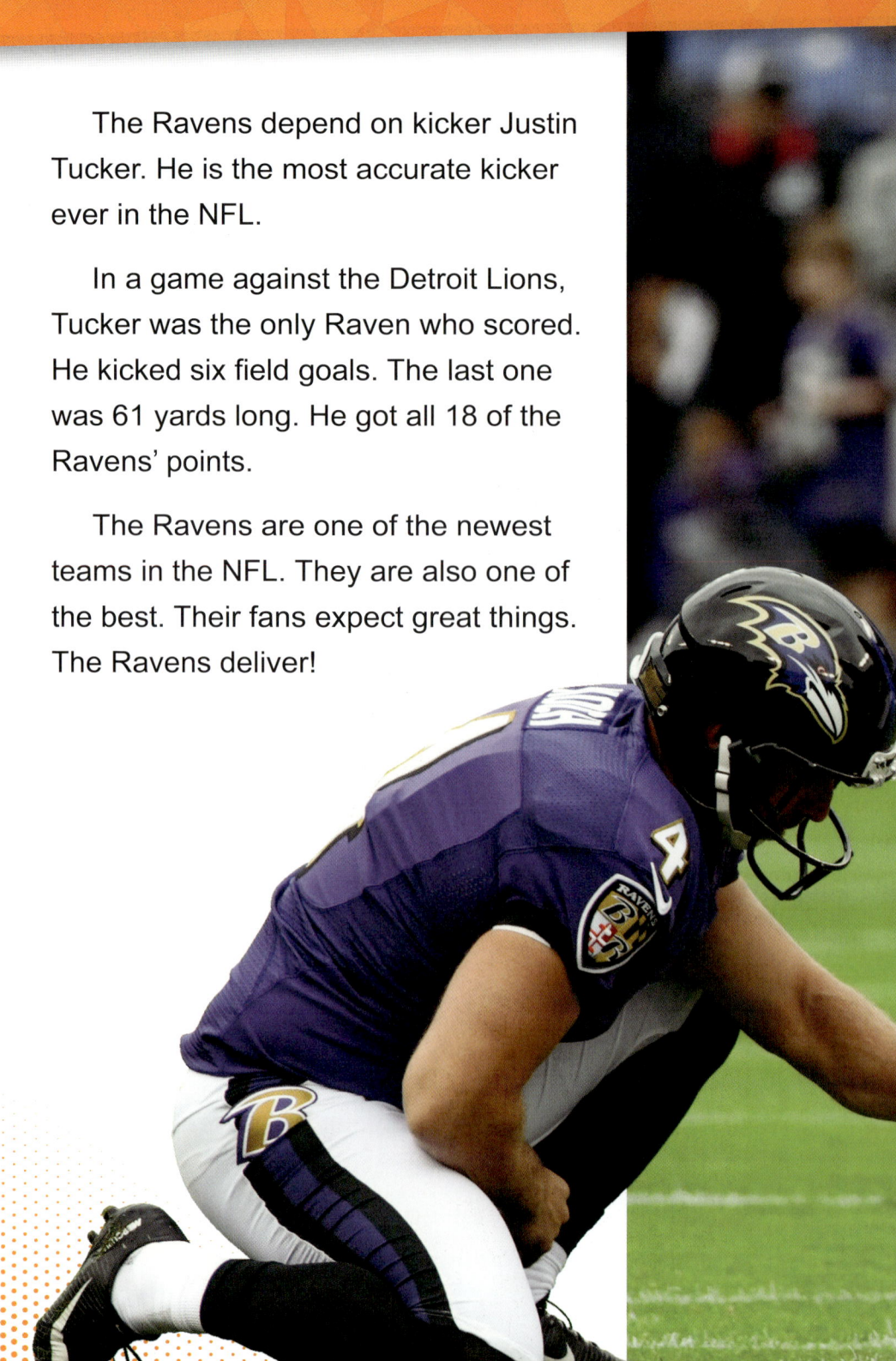

Justin Tucker

BEYOND THE BOOK

After reading the book, it's time to think about what you learned. Try the following exercises to jumpstart your ideas.

RESEARCH

FIND OUT MORE. Where would you go to find out more about your favorite NFL teams and players? Check out NFL.com, of course. Each team also has its own website. What other sports information sites can you find? See if you can find other cool facts about your favorite team.

CREATE

GET ARTISTIC. Each NFL team has a logo. The Ravens logo shows a black bird. Get some art materials and try designing your own Ravens logo. Or create a new team and make a logo for it. What colors would you choose? How would you draw the mascot?

DISCOVER

GO DEEP! As this book shows, Ravens QB Lamar Jackson is a special talent. He can pass for lots of TDs, but he can also run like a running back. Find some other QBs from the past and today who were also two-way threats. What skills did they share? How were they different?

GROW

GET OUT AND PLAY! You don't need to be in the NFL to enjoy football. You just need a football and some friends. Play touch or tag football. Or you can hang cloth flags from your belt; grab the belt and make the "tackle." See who has the best arm to be quarterback. Who is the best receiver? Who can run the fastest? Time to play football!

RESEARCH NINJA

Visit www.ninjaresearcher.com/2206 to learn how to take your research skills and book report writing to the next level!

RESEARCH

DIGITAL LITERACY TOOLS

SEARCH LIKE A PRO
Learn about how to use search engines to find useful websites.

FACT OR FAKE?
Discover how you can tell a trusted website from an untrustworthy resource.

TEXT DETECTIVE
Explore how to zero in on the information you need most.

SHOW YOUR WORK
Research responsibly—learn how to cite sources.

WRITE

GET TO THE POINT
Learn how to express your main ideas.

PLAN OF ATTACK
Learn prewriting exercises and create an outline.

DOWNLOADABLE REPORT FORMS

Further Resources

BOOKS

Fishman, Jon M. *Lamar Jackson (Sports All-Stars)*. Minneapolis, MN: Lerner, 2020.

Price, Karen. *Steelers vs. Ravens (NFL Rivalries)*. Mankato, MN: North Star Editions, 2019.

Whiting, Jim. *Baltimore Ravens (Inside the NFL)*. Mankato, MN: Creative Paperbacks, 2019.

WEBSITES

Factsurfer.com gives you a safe, fun way to find more information.

1. Go to www.factsurfer.com.
2. Enter "Baltimore Ravens" into the search box and click
3. Select your book cover to see a list of related websites.

Glossary

draft: NFL event at which teams choose college players. Marquise Brown was the Ravens' No. 1 draft pick in 2019.

Heisman Trophy: award for the top college player in the nation. Mark Ingram scored 17 touchdowns for Alabama and won the Heisman Trophy in 2009.

interceptions: passes caught by the defense. Baltimore's Ed Reed was an expert in making interceptions.

overtime: extra time played after a 60-minute game ends in a tie. Baltimore tied the game 10–10 and won in overtime 13–10.

rookie: a player in his or her first pro season. Jaylon Ferguson started at linebacker for Baltimore in his rookie season.

sacked: when a quarterback is tackled behind the line of scrimmage. Matt Judon sacked Tom Brady and the Patriots lost nine yards.

safety: a defensive position that covers receivers. Ed Reed was one of the best safeties in NFL history.

veteran: a player with more than a couple of seasons of action. Mark Ingram is a veteran after eight NFL seasons.

Index

Baltimore Colts, 6
Billick, Brian, 8
Boulware, Peter, 8
Cincinnati Bengals, 20
Cleveland Browns, 18
Denver Broncos, 10
Detroit Lions, 26
Flacco, Joe, 10, 14, 20
Harbaugh, Jim, 14
Harbaugh, John, 10, 14
Ingram, Mark, 24
Jackson, Lamar, 12, 22, 24, 25
Jones, Jacoby, 10
Judon, Matt, 25
Lewis, Jamal, 8, 18
Lewis, Ray, 8, 17
New York Giants, 6, 9
Ogden, Jonathan, 8, 16, 25
Poe, 4
Reed, Ed, 18
San Francisco 49ers, 14
Seattle Seahawks, 18
Suggs, Terrell, 20
Super Bowl, 4, 9, 10, 14, 17, 18
Tennessee Titans, 12
Tucker, Justin, 10, 26
Unitas, Johnny, 6
Yanda, Marshal, 25

PHOTO CREDITS

The images in this book are reproduced through the courtesy of: AP Images: Dave Hammond 6; Matt Slocum 15. Focus on Football: 12, 16, 17, 18, 23, 24, 25. Newscom: Mark Goldman/Icon SW 4; David Berman/KRT 8; Mark Reis/MCT 10; Kevin Dietsch/UPI 14, 20; George Bridges/KRT 19. **Cover photo:** Focus on Football.

About the Author

Diane Bailey has written dozens of books for kids and teens, on everything from sports to science to civil rights. She has two grown sons and lives with her husband in Kansas, where they like to watch football, talk about football, argue about football, and look forward to more football!